Disney LEARNING

PIXAR

PHONICS
COLLECTION

Short Vowels

Scholastic Inc.

All rights reserved. Published by Scholastic Inc., *Publishers since 1920*. SCHOLASTIC and associated logos are trademarks and/or registered trademarks of Scholastic Inc.

The publisher does not have any control over and does not assume any responsibility for author or third-party websites or their content.

This book is a work of fiction. Names, characters, places, and incidents are either the product of the author's imagination or are used fictitiously, and any resemblance to actual persons, living or dead, business establishments, events, or locales is entirely coincidental.

ISBN 978-1-338-76318-8

10 9 8 7 6 5 4 3 2 1   21 22 23 24 25

Printed in the U.S.A.   40

First printing 2021

Book design by Two Red Shoes Design

Rat in a Hat

This story is filled with lots of **short -a** words, which appear in bold type. Here are some to sound out with your child.

at	hand	pan
bad	has	plan
can	hat	rat
catch	man	that

You can also work with your child to identify the **short -a** sound in these longer words, which do not appear in bold.

imagine   natural   spatula

BOOK 1

Look **at that rat!**

That rat has a spatula.

That rat can use a **pan**.

That rat is a natural!

Look **at that man**!

That man can not cook.

That man's food
is very **bad**.

Look! **That man can catch that rat.**

The **man has** a **plan.**

The **rat can** give him a **hand**!

The **rat** helps the **man**.

The **man** learns from the **rat**.

The **man** hides the **rat**...

in his **hat**!

Imagine **that**!

ONWARD
The Best Quest

Disney · PIXAR

This story is filled with lots of **short -e** words, which appear in bold type. Here are some to sound out with your child.

best	get	spell
check	head	them
dead	help	then
end	leg	well
friend	quest	
gem	set	

Ian and Barley are brothers.
They do not **get** along.

Their mom gives **them**
a **spell** and a **gem**.
These will **help them**
see their dad.

Ian casts the **spell**.
Look! It is dad's **legs**!

Then, the **gem** breaks.
Dad has no **head**.
He is just **legs**!

The brothers **set** off on a **quest**.
They must find a new **gem**.

First, they **get** to the Manticore.
She has a map to a new **gem**!

The brothers **head** off.
Barley **checks** the map.

Oh no! A **dead end**!
Ian uses a **spell** to **get** across.

The map leads **them** to a **well**.
They **head** in.

They follow the water.
Ian practices his **spells**.

At the **end** of the tunnel, Barley finds the **gem**!

But the **gem** is cursed.
A dragon tries to **get** Barley!

Ian uses a **spell**
to **get** to the dragon.

Another **spell helps** Barley
see their dad.
Ian can not **get** out to see him.

In the **end**, they have each other.
Ian and Barley are not just family.
They are **best friends**.

Disney · PIXAR
Cars

The Big Win

This story is filled with lots of **short -i** words, which appear in bold type. Here are some to sound out with your child.

begin	his	still
big	hit	this
did	into	trick
ditch	is	will
finish	pit	win
fix	quick	winner
give	quit	winning
him	spin	

This is Lightning McQueen.

He wants to **win** the **big** race.

This is Chick Hicks.
He wants to **win** the **big** race.

This is the King.
He wants to **win** the **big** race.

The race **begins**!

But who **will win**?

The King and Chick Hicks
are going to **win**!

Lightning **is** last.
But he **will** not **quit**!

Lightning pulls **into his pit**.

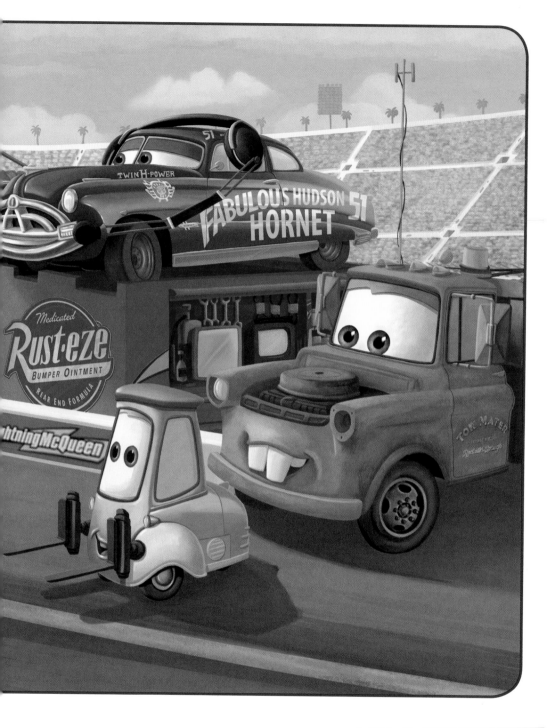

His crew **gives him** a **quick fix**.

Chick Hicks cheats.
He **hits** the King!

The King **spins into** a **ditch**.

Lightning does not like
Chick's **trick**.
The King was **winning**!

Lightning **quits** the race.
He helps the King to the
finish.

Lightning **did** not **win** the **big** race. But Lightning **is** still a **winner**!

A Great Job

BOOK 4
Short -o

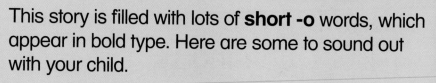

This story is filled with lots of **short -o** words, which appear in bold type. Here are some to sound out with your child.

hot	lot	sob
job	not	stomp
knob	shot	stop

Riley does **not** feel so **hot**.
She **sobs**.

Her Emotions try to help.
It is **not** an easy **job**.

Sadness takes a **shot**.
She does **not** do the **job**.

Disgust does **not** try so hard. She does **not** do the **job**.

Anger **stomps** in.
He does **not** do the **job**.

Fear turns some **knobs**.
He does **not** do the **job**.

Joy does **not** do the **job**.

The Emotions fight a **lot**.
But they do **not** do the **job**.

Then they **stop**.
They work together.
They do a great **job**!

Study Up

This story is filled with lots of **short -u** words, which appear in bold type. Here are some to sound out with your child.

but	fun	study
club	just	up
dunk	must	

Mike shows **up** at monster school.
He wants to **study**, **study**, **study**.

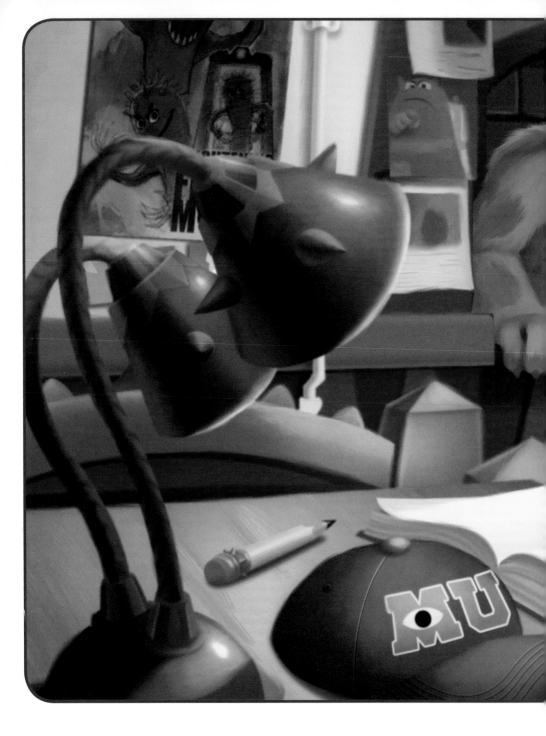

Sulley shows **up** at monster school.

He wants to have **fun**, **fun**, **fun**.

Mike knows he **must** work hard.

He cleans **up** his room.

Mike knows he **must** make friends.

He signs **up** for a **club**.

Sulley knows he **must** work hard.

But he **just** wants to have **fun**.

Sulley **just** plays games.
He does not **study**.

Mike takes time to **study**.
He knows he **must**.

Mike gets a slam **dunk**!
Now that's **fun**.

Short Vowel Activities

The following pages contain activities to practice comprehension of short vowel sounds. As you go through the activities with your child, encourage them to sound out the words and say their answers out loud.

Find the Words

Remy the **rat** hides in Linguini's **hat**. **Rat** and **hat** both have the **short -a** sound. Can you find and point to any other **short -a** words in this picture?

Hint: Look for the words
pan, man, and **hand.**

Imagine That!

Imagine and **that** have the **short -a** sound. Remy **imagines that** he **can** cook with a **pan**. What do you imagine? Come up with a story using the words below. Try to use at least one **short -a** word in every sentence.

bat   **slam**   **cats**

hands   **ran**   **happy**

Complete the Path

Help Barley **get** away from the pest! Point to only the boxes that have **short -e** words in them.

best	eat	beat	hear	meet	year
egg	help	let	see	eel	meat
heat	heed	nest	near	neat	feet
team	free	net	pest	rest	tell
heap	mean	feel	tree	key	test
leap	sheep	peep	meal	deep	yet

Find the Rhyme

Use your finger to draw a line between the **short -e** rhyming words. The first one has been done for you.

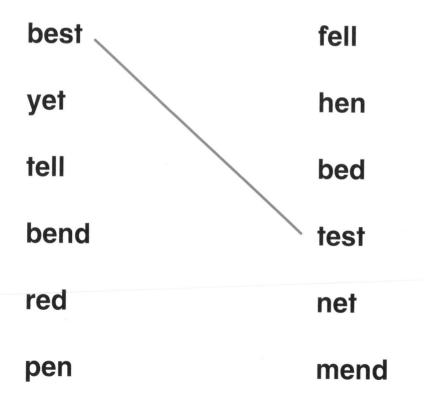

best	fell
yet	hen
tell	bed
bend	test
red	net
pen	mend

Finish to Win

Lightning McQueen wants a **big win**.
Can you help **him** cross the **finish** line?
Follow the **short -i** words with your finger
to complete the maze.

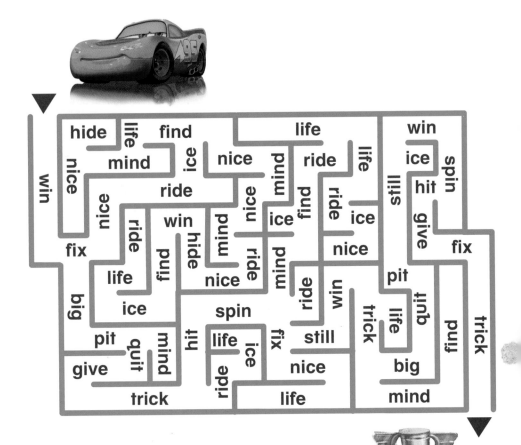

Words in the Way

When there **is** something in the way, **winning** can be **tricky**, even for Lightning McQueen. Read the words below and point to all the boxes that do <u>not</u> have a **short -i** sound.

trick	bet	find
time	race	spin
hit	car	speed
rock	ride	kid
pit	win	up

What a Job!

Riley's Emotions have a **job** to do. It is **not** an easy **job**. **Not** and **job** are both **short -o** words. Can you point to the names of jobs below that also have the **short -o** sound?

cop

coach

doctor

host

coder

logger

What job would you like to have when you grow up?

Hot or Cold?

Hot is a **short -o** word.

Read each word below out loud. Point to all the words that have the **short -o** sound.

HOT

go	not	job	no
stop	home	lot	slow

Study Up!

Mike **studies** hard at Monsters University. Sulley does not. He just wants to have **fun**. **Study** and **fun** are both **short -u** words.

Read the words below. Are any of the words something you must do every day? Are any of them something you do for fun? Point to all of the activities that have a word with a **short -u** sound.

nap	**dance**
help	**brush**
run	**hum**

Find Short -U Words

Can you point to the **short -u** words in the boxes below?

cold	job	dull	rule	lunch
dunk	true	win	rat	human
hide	snack	study	scare	just
rest	flunk	not	get	hat
party	fun	try	bug	cute

Make Your Own Word

Can you read the short vowel words below? Now come up with your own! Say your new words out loud. Try to think of a word for each short vowel sound.

short -a   rat   _____

short -e   egg   _____

short -i   win   _____

short -o   job   _____

short -u   up   _____

Short Vowels

Short Vowel Hunt

Look at the word list below. Read the words and identify the sounds they make. Point to the short vowel words.

big	pan	pit	rub
huge	ice	yet	hot
hope	hat	ape	heat
job	wet	aim	hug

You Did It!

Now you know your short vowel sounds. Read these stories again and again for even more phonics fun! You'll be a reading superstar in no time!